PLATE PIES

●●●●●●

by

ALAN MARKLAND

AuthorHouse™
1663 Liberty Drive, Suite 200
Bloomington, IN 47403
www.authorhouse.com
Phone: 1-800-839-8640

AuthorHouse™ UK Ltd.
500 Avebury Boulevard
Central Milton Keynes, MK9 2BE
www.authorhouse.co.uk
Phone: 08001974150

First published by AuthorHouse 8/3/2006

ISBN: 1-4259-4499-X (sc)

Printed in the United States of America
Bloomington, Indiana

This book is printed on acid-free paper.

Cover by Ian Markland

My thanks and appreciations are due to my proof reader, critic and comforter, Christine who, handily, lives with me.

Table of Contents

ALICE

●●●●●●●●●●●●●

The last time I saw her she had new stockings on.

'Fifteen denier,' she kept on telling me. 'Twelve and six from Woolworth's.' It had been her birthday a couple of days before; seventeen. She had treated herself. She would look over her shoulder and down at her leg, bent at the knee.

'Is my seam straight?' she'd ask.

I'll always remember. She'd be five months by then. You couldn't tell though, she was that small. Just a bit flushed in her cheeks, like she had rouge on, only light. Not red I mean. Suited her it did, a bit of colour. She never wore make-up. No need, you know? Her lips were – well – they were very nice. Her eyes too, only I cannot remember the colour of them. She used to say that my eyes were the best thing about me. She liked my hair too but not combed. Always ruffling it.

'That's better,' she would say giving it a flick with her hand. Little hands, she had. Very pale. You could see the veins through. Blue and her heart beating at the wrist. She was clean. Smelled clean I mean. Not soapy or lavender or any of them. Even her breath. Fresh. Her hair was long usually. Right down her back. Straight, shiny. She used to sit on it to make me laugh. She'd had it cut short by then though, for strength she said and she was eating well. Not that you would notice. A bird could put away more.

'Feeding for two now,' she would say, nibbling a chip, her eyes sparkling. I used to think she had been crying, they could be that soft and bright sometimes. I never saw her cry, not properly. Funny that, you'd have thought she would.

She lived in the same village as me. Her dad, mam, her twin sister and Jimmy, the youngest. A family like any other. They kept themselves to themselves, as we all did. It was the way. Her father was a railwayman and he was on the committee at the works club. Popular he was, with his mates and that. A big man, always laughing and joking around.

'A bit of a lad,' my mother said. 'She has a lot to put up with,' meaning his wife. I never took much notice. I didn't like him somehow but I put that down to him not thinking much of me.

'Keep away from our lass.' He had said and I knew the reason for that. I was always a bit slow you see. Not daft or anything, though there were some as thought so.

'Has difficulty,' they said at school. 'Learning.' It was a toss up at one time whether I went to the Special same as Bobby Fogg who had fits. Me and him got on well enough but I was glad I wasn't classed the same. Actually, I had always found being a bit thick comfortable. Folk left you alone, didn't expect much. My girl didn't mind and that's all I cared about really.

She would never talk much about home. Once or twice she would say:

'We are all going on holiday shortly,' or 'Father's thinking of taking us to the circus.' They never went. You didn't see them having visitors either, you know, for tea or anything. She told me that they read a lot, played games, told each other stories. I used to imagine them sitting around a table, laughing. Together, a family like you see sometimes in those advertisements for bed-time drinks. We could have been like that. Her and me. Some nights when the ward is quiet and there's just that green light on at the end where the nurse sits, I lie thinking how it would be. Me with my pipe – I don't smoke actually but I could take it up. I would be doing the bills perhaps and she would be brushing our daughter's hair, putting plaits in. The boy playing with the cat by the fire. I do a lot of that, imagining. Sometimes I think I catch a glimpse of her, only it turns out to be one of the nurses, or a patient perhaps. You know, how they flick their hair back, one side and then the other. Just like she used to. I get a little jolt when they do that, as if my heart has been squeezed.

'We could manage.' I remember her saying. I remember that almost better than anything else. You could never tell what she was thinking though. Never. I mean, usually, with people, if they are telling you something and you look, you can near enough see if they mean it or not by the way their face goes. Not with her though. She had a look all the time as if she knew something, a secret. Well, of course, after what happened, when it all came out, it sort of clicked. But it was more than that. You know them pictures you see? Where Jesus' mother is holding him and he has nothing on and there are usually some angels and a few saints or something, looking, and she is just sat, arm around him? It's like a smile but sad too. Happy and unhappy at the same time. I've never made it out yet. Even after all the time I have been in here. Thirty odd years now and that's a while back. I've never blamed myself though. Not for any of it really. Things just happened. I often think, if it had been different, if we had got married when she said. But I suppose I would always have been thinking; whose kid is it? Who gave her that baby? And we had never even done it. We had never – well, a kiss and that. Once she let me touch her, under her blouse. Like a bird it was, a little soft bird, warm and breathing in my hand. She kissed me too at the same time. Then stopped me.

'Hush.' She said, very quiet, like you would to a child. Funny what you remember, little things like that. But we never did anything, so I knew. I should have said something, asked her. I just couldn't get it out. I thought, well, what everyone else thought. It was one of the others. Jimmy Greenhalgh. Tom Whatsisname.

You know? They were always after her. Got her down once on the grass, behind the swings in Lever Edge Park. I just stood there, watching. They had her legs open. Laughing they were and poking their fingers in her. Pulling and snatching. She never screamed, just got her teeth in Jimmy's ear and bit. Wouldn't let go. Shaking and tearing like a little terrier. He screamed blue murder and the others ran off. She spit his blood right in his face, then went home. She never even looked at me. Anyway, that was before. When she asked for us to get married that day, just after her birthday, I didn't answer her. I just stared at the kids playing ball. I'd a good excuse anyway. I had been called up and would be going away to do my National Service.

'It's alright Mick.' She said, like she was saying goodnight or pass the sugar or something. Then she went up the hill, by where the bridge used to be, under them trees. I thought she would turn, wave but she didn't. It was the last time I saw her.

Septic, it was that killed her. They say she stuck a wire up and twisted it all in her. I was in Aldershot at the time, commando training course. They let me home for the funeral. My mother had told them we were engaged and that's when I knew. At the grave, as they lowered her in, jerking them ropes and the rain coming down. Someone had an umbrella over the vicar and I could hear him, knew it was prayers and that, but no words. Only the drone of his voice, up and down. Then, just as the folk started throwing flowers in and hands full of dirt, I looked up, straight into the eyes of her father and I knew. I didn't need the rest of it – what happened later. It was as if I had been told. Right at the grave-side. Her own father.

I didn't do anything; it was like I was cold all over. So cold I thought I would never get warm again. It was six years later when I did it.

I loved the army. It suited me. A lot of the lads complained all the time. The discipline.The bull. It hurt them to be shouted at. Not me, I lapped it up. I never got any stripes, though I was always first over the assault course and that. Naming of parts, in weaponry, was like poetry to me. Unarmed combat, sports. The exams though, where you had to put it all down on paper – well I was no good at that. But it didn't matter; they liked me, sergeants and so on.

'Good soldier material,' they said. 'Does as he is told.'

After my initial training I got sent to Singapore and then the Korean War broke out and I was taken prisoner. They called it brain-washing what they did to us. Beatings and the lights on all the time. I never knew what day it was or whether it was day or night for eighteen months. You'd get solitary for a week or more at a time. Locked up in a box no bigger than a coffin. They'd put a bucket on your head; bang it with a stick until you thought your brains would blow up. Questions, questions. Broken bones, dysentery, men dying. They would give us copies, doctored, of the English newspapers. Looked just like the real thing they did and we would read of things that were supposed to be happening back home. Things to upset us. Make us think we had been forgotten, that England and America were losing the war and we might as well give up, agree to everything they said. I had been there about two years when I saw the article. In one of the Sunday papers it was, provided by the Red Cross. It was all about him, how he had been convicted of doing things to his own four year old boy and to Sally, my girl's twin. Their mother had seen it all and done nothing.

Later on at the murder trial, they said, after tests, that I was unfit to plead. That my mind had gone what with the indoctrination and the beatings. Living with it all that time, festering, waiting. I got him after he came out of prison. Three years they gave him and never even mentioned Alice. It was as if she had never existed. Three years and he only did two for good behaviour.

He had just left the Royal Oak on Bradshawgate. I followed him on his way home, down by the canal. I slit his throat, just like I had been taught in the army. What you do is, you put your left hand over his head from behind, push a finger into an eye-socket and pull back sharp. The knife-point goes in just under the angle of the left mandible, immediately below the ear. A vertical thrust drives it up behind the condyle. With that as a fixed point and the larynx as a fulcrum, lever back towards yourself. The larynx, being cartilage, will crack easily and allow access to the jugular veins and the carotids. A sweeping cut to the right will sever one or all of these and death will be quiet and certain.

It worked perfectly, until right at the last moment. His legs had gone and I knew he had had it but I wanted to see. I wanted him to see me and know as he died. I wanted him to suffer and to take his suffering with him. So I turned him as he fell and that's when I got the blood on me. They said I cut bits of him off, parts and that but I don't remember it. They are probably right though what with all this blood. I wash it off two or three times a day but it seeps out again. Red, smelling of iron, running down. I wish I could remember the colour of her eyes.

A FLY IN THE OINTMENT

●●●●●●●●●●●●●

Alfred Pilkington loved his wife, Elsie; adored her, every inch. There were not all that many; inches that is and that had been the first thing that had attracted him to her, all those years ago. Her small-ness. So neat she was, uncluttered. Just enough of everything and no exaggerations.

He had grown up in a house filled with girls, four sisters. Big sisters, lumbering about in their size nine shoes. There had been things – strange articles of female apparel – strung up, drip, drip, drying over the bath. Voluminous, tent- like contrivances that, in the books that he read were supposed to be delicate, intimate. His sister's smalls were as delicate as tarpaulins on the backs of articulated trucks.

She loved him back, Elsie, worshipped him. Sweethearts since childhood when they had counted the cost of a seat on the back row of the Regal. Setting up in business together – scrap metal. Prospering, making their fortune and now, finally, retiring to their Greek island to enjoy it all in their autumn years.

There was of course, a fly in the ointment, there always is and he had managed to be philosophical about it down the years. It irritated him, true, drove him wild sometimes, deep down, hidden. The indignity. He swore, each time she did it that he would have it out with her, tell her once and for all but then, his better nature and the thought of hurting her, his dear one, stopped him. Tolerance, that's all it needed. And love.

Elsie smoked. That's what it was. He didn't of course. Never had. It was a silly waste of good money in the first place and then, when he had made his pile and did not have to count cost – well – life was just too good to be shortened.

It was not just the fags – and it was not the money certainly. It was the way she lit them, that was what did it. Furtive best describes her actions, furtive and quick. Thirty two times in every day – he had counted – there would be the click of the clasp on her handbag, a rustling of silver paper, the tap-tap-tapping of fag on carton, the striking of the match – always away from herself and with a strong, almost savage downward movement. Then – worst of all, the inhalation. A sharp drawing in. A mingling of tobacco, paper, and sulphurous match fume, producing an awful miasma, a stinking, choking fug that, straightaway and in one great blast she would exhale – directly into Alfred's cringing, expectant face.

'Sorry – sorry.' She would always apologize. Wafting away the stench with a delicate hand. 'Sorry love,' she would say. 'Oh dear. I always do it. Do forgive me,' and he did. Of course he did. He loved her.

They were sitting by the fountain in Syntagma Square in central Athens. It was one of their favourite spots, handy for their hotel and just beneath the Palace. Sipping their mocha, they gazed contentedly into each other's eyes. Her hand, small, pretty, perfumed, met his every now and again in a passing touch that thrilled them both by its familiarity and promise. Their glances, always and only for each other, sent and received identical messages of togetherness, comfort and desire. And then she lit up.

It will never be known what unfortunate circumstances conspired at that particular time and in that particular place to produce such a terrible result.

Of all the fags over all the years, in bad and in good times, the question why this one? will always remain unanswered. Suffice to say, Alfred went ballistic.

'Ungrateful cow. Disgusting worm. Foul-breathed slut.' These, perhaps the more benign epithets Fred slung at her, shook her to the core and stopped her in mid drag. The crowd were hushed suddenly at the spectacle and then, nodding and nudging each other they told how well they knew the couple, had dined with them and so on, enjoying, as crowds do, their connection, however slight with another persons tragedy.

Elsie sat, head lowered, cigarette smouldering, unpuffed, between her slender, now trembling fingers. Alfred, of course was already ashamed. The tirade now spent, colouring returned to normal, spittle wiped from the corners of his mouth, he stood dismayed at what he done.

Elsie, gathering up her various accessories and without a word, got up and crossed the road to their hotel.

'You are right,' she told him next morning at breakfast. 'I have been selfish and a beast. I will stop. In fact,' and here she made a small gesture of dismissal. 'I have stopped. I will never smoke again.' And true to her word she did not.

Life, however, was never the same. It went on, as lives do but something, a vital spark, a secret ingredient, was missing and the loss, which they both knew could never be made good, was a sadness, a terrible pain to both of them.

And then came the chocolates.

Alfred had noticed a thickening, hardly perceptible at first, about his wife's hitherto slender waist. There was a vague puffiness under the eyes. Her rings, he now saw, were dug in and had begun to burrow into the soft flesh of her fingers. Her watchstrap, Cartier, solid gold, becoming almost lost in a pink, meaty fold.

Coloured paper, empty boxes, brown stained tissues, littered their apartments. Their bed was taken over, excluding him, by rustlings; the sharp crackle of cellophane and a munch, slurp, crunch as she waded like a pelican through one pound, four pounds, seven pounds of raisin-filled, almond-spiced, fruit-soaked, nut-charged pralines, roulades, caramels, mallows and, watching her, Alfred, reminded of pigs snuffling truffles, retired to a spare room, leaving her to it.

All through the winter she gorged, ballooning as she went. Her eyes – alone amongst her attributes that never lost their beauty – peered now pathetically from the uttermost depths of her over-lapping cheeks.

Her mouth, lip-sticked still, stained brown, appeared like a small, over-ripe raspberry in the burgeoning mounds of her deathly pale face.

The end, when it came, had a sound to it. Not a bang exactly, nor yet a plop. Perhaps a mixture of the two. The sort of noise that a brown paper bag might make, filled with tepid water and splattered by a fist in the palm of a hand.

Alfred, dozing in the anteroom, was awakened by the noise and knew instinctively what it was. He was not prepared, however, for the sight that greeted him as he opened the door and went in. Elsie had exploded. Her several orifices, trapped shut by invading flesh, had caused a combustion internally and she was spread, distributed almost evenly in lumps and in gobbets about the pink and blue décor of the bedroom. Dripping, gurgling and with little wisps of steam here and there wafting, she hung in festoons, like a mad artist's nightmare before his horror stricken eyes.

Alfred began to gibber. His hair turned immediately white and he fell to the floor in a dead faint. He awoke restrained. His arms locked across his chest in a strange, white, canvas jacket.

'Hi there,' the man said, face beaming, looming over him.

'I am Steve – your friend for life and I am here to take good care of you from here on in.' The ash, an inch and a quarter long, dangled precariously from the end of the cigarette as Steve, removing it briefly from his kindly smiling mouth, blew a perfectly formed smoke ring straight and full into Alfred's trapped, upturned face.

GOING GENTLE

● ● ● ● ● ● ● ● ● ● ● ● ●

The pain would not come yet. An hour at least before the panic, the clammy sweat. He was hot already but that was normal, healthy after the walk. What a walk. More like a route march with obstacles. Dry-stone walls, centuries old, criss-crossing the rough landscape, seemingly without design. Their primary purpose lost in time, part now of the nature of the moor.

He rested against the stone slabs. Granite worn to the wind, black from the smoke of long gone mills; gritty under his palms.

The town sprawled below him, cupped in its bowl, backed by purple-gorsed hills. A curlew sang, looping, low, and here, nestled in the lee of the wall – shaded, strong stems, topped by milk-white froth – his reward. The goal he had set himself. Wild Chrysanthemums they had called them, though he was sure there was no relation. They were less pretty than shop-bought ones, dead as soon as cut and the roots strangely addictive, more-ish people said, although bitter to the taste. He found a strong stick and began to dig, allowing the memories to flood in.

Running wild on young, strong legs, stained by winberries, blown by the wind, scoured and scratched by thicket and bramble. 'Spare a drink of water?' they would ask the farmer, who gave them milk, like as not, straight from the cooler and the cow.

The earth, sweet-rotten, tumbled away as he foraged, easy as the years since the last time. Following the stem as it changed green to white, careful not to lose it, deeper he went, a foot or more and then he paused, mopped his brow, breath a bit harder, determined.

He leaned his back against the strong wall, full of the smells and the sounds of the moorland. A plover nearby now, wing-dragging, crying false lame-song away from the nest and the young. There were skylarks tumbling. A cow bellowed fields away and, up from the town, a child's cry; sudden, shrill on the wind as he dozed.

The first stab came just as he stirred. Twisting, piercing, gripping tight on his rib cage. Cruel fingers forced bones apart as, with a trembling hand he placed the pill beneath his tongue. Waves of nausea flooded him. He could hear the thump of his own heartbeat.

Relax, he told himself. He knew it worked. The pain would ease. Relax. While every sinew cried revolt. Through the mist of stinging tears, indistinct by the edge of the field below, his eye caught a movement. He blinked and the movement took shape, advancing up the slope towards him.

She was about twenty, the girl, by the looks of her. Slim, she wore a green trilby hat, beneath which flowed her hair, dark, shimmering. A sleek black waterfall. She led, short-bridled, a small white pony which nuzzled her neck as they came. Her eyes were blue he saw, just like his own and they fixed, not blinking, on his. Coming up close, the sun behind them, girl and horse, she spoke.

'He found you – didn't you Sam?'

Kissing the pony's muzzle, eyeing the part dug plant. 'Well – he found something any road up – he likes them, the roots.' Then she dropped the reigns, allowing the horse to graze.

He told her he was staying nearby, at The Dog in the village.

'Lived here once – as a boy.'

'Yes.' She said, head on one side waiting.

'Here – have a nut,' and she smiled at him, a strange, sad, happy smile.

The plane was on them suddenly, out of nowhere. The big, black shadow of it dancing over the fields. There was a blast, a screaming of turbines, the hammer-blow impact as it banked flying over them, low on the forest, into the dale, white stream trailing as, with a final roar, it shot out of sight below the hills.

'Tornado,' he told her. 'Pan Avia. GR4. Down from Wharton I expect,' and he watched her as she scraped with her thumbnail the soft-skinned roots.

Offering him one as their eyes met and held.

Back at the pub, he made himself comfortable at the bar.

'Never heard of her,' The landlord said, creamy suds billowing around the pint pot as he pulled.

'Gypsy was she? Only you get all sorts up yon nowadays. Happen she's from the farm. I heard they were taking on – tater bashing like. Here, get by that fire – I'll fetch you your ale.'

He was glad he had come. It had all worked out. Even this, the pub. Black Dog – just as it had been all those years ago. He sat by the blaze among worn, polished wood, cracked black beams, firelight on warm brass, the soft regular thud and murmur of darts in the taproom.

'Get out of this heat,' they had told him, grounded in Delhi.

There would be no going back. It was over now. So final.

'Six months,' the quack said. 'Best make the most of it.'

And it had been this place, of all others, that he had been drawn to, immediately, as if by magnet. There had been no debate, he had obeyed the pull. Sipping his beer he stared deep into the flames of orange – blue, deep roaring red. A bubble of sap, trapped in the blaze burst abruptly sending a shower of sparks, golden, glimmering up into the dark maw of the chimney and he heard again, in his memory, the sweet, sharp hiss as the rockets, dispatched by his thumb, streaked straight to their target of mean mud huts. The fireball. Children running. The old woman, hand raised to the horror of it, knee deep amongst the paddy. Innocent.

He shook his head. Sipped again at his drink. Forty years give or take, and here he was back in his own backyard. And now he knew why. It had been the plane that had done it, earlier today, up on the moor. And the girl, standing there. It had taken him right back again over all the years.

There had been the stink of candle smoke, stale piss and damp concrete. Babies sobbed on mothers' comforting breasts. They had sat helpless, huddled, eyes skyward, scared. There was a stillness, as if the air had frozen. He remembered the tin hat on the head of the man opposite. A.R.P. It said in white letters. Air Raid Police - and the gas mask neat on his shoulder.

There had been a slow drone overhead. A throbbing.

'Junkers.' He had whispered, soft in her ear. 'Eighty Eight's – one day I will fly one something like it.'

'Yes,' she had told him, squeezing his hand. 'Yes, love, you will.'

She had been the eldest, by two full minutes. Leading him easily, if noisily, into the world.

'Came that fast,' their mother would tell folk. 'Like two little fat peas – plop, plop. Fourteen pounds between them and me thinking three weeks to go.'

The air raid had interrupted their party. Tiny candles, six pink, six blue, on a snow white cake. Funny hats, laughter, blind man's buff, then the bombs came and they had run hand in hand to the shelter.

He could not remember them pulling her away. She had been cold. She had cried. Then she was gone. The steel joist, he was later told, had broken her back. Three days it took to dig them out, her frail form protecting his.

'When you get your first wages,' She had said in the dark. 'You can buy me a pony, a white one and I will give you lifts home on your weekends.'

It had been as if she had been amputated. Sliced from him as a leg would have been and for the rest of his life he had never felt whole. He had caught glimpses of her over the years, in other girl's eyes. A gesture, shocking, unexpected in crowds. Her hand on his shoulder that night over Hong Kong, coming in to land at Kai Tak with the landing gear jammed.

The quiet assurance of her presence, fleeting, imagined? And now he was sure.

His room was warm, welcoming as he entered. A soft patchwork quilt over clean, white sheets. In darkness he saw the moon, cold, white, framed in the windowpane. Wind sighed gently in the leaves of nearby trees. The moor was hushed. Down below, in the cobbled yard, he heard the sharp clip of hooves, bright steel on polished stones.

Closing his eyes as the pain began, he smiled and went to sleep.

GREEN MOSS

•••••••••••••

The nicks between the cobbles are filled with moss the colour of emeralds. It is silky to the touch and lovely. Without roots it is easily wrenched from its moorings, with only a soft sucking sound in protest. There is a foul smell as the underside is revealed, black, filthy, dripping.

Patrick lies prone, an eye lined up with a strip of the moss, the other eye is closed, beginning to swell. Blood seeps from a split lip, mingling with the rain as he bites down hard to savour the hurt and the shame.

'And stay out.' His father had yelled, but he will not leave him there long – afraid the neighbours will see.

'Up – up. Fight you bloody Jessie.' As the jabs came in the kidneys, followed by the old one two and Patrick was down. Out-fought by the skill and brute strength of this one time fair - ground pugilist. Patrick is twelve years old and a disappointment to his father.

Kneeling at the blue upholstered rail of the children's chapel, he watches the weak sunlight as it seeps through the cold stone window frames behind the high altar. Baby angels, well fed by the looks of it, dance contentedly in the coloured light. An old man – God by all accounts, white beard on, wreathed in clouds, points a long bony finger and drills a fierce eye straight through Pat's jersey and into his soul.

The church is empty save for one young woman. One of the clique. The chosen ones. Holy and clean. She arranges the lilies for no reward. Goes home to her hubby who tells her what a lousy day he has had at the office while she pours hot, juicy gravy over a brimming plate. They will sit by the wireless in the evening, her head in his lap as they savour their Ovaltine, in twin matching mugs, for a good nights sleep and the health that it brings. Their kids will be rosy. Purple-edged bibles with a gold thread to show where they are up to, clutched tightly in Sunday scrubbed hands. They smile, nod, and say 'How do?' to the vicar who ruffles their hair with a lily-white hand, assuring them places in heaven.

His own hands steepled, Patrick watches as the woman sighs softly, contentedly, bows to the altar and leaves. He follows her out into the street. It is still raining.

The spare ground by the side of the Lad's Club in Mount Street is be-decked in coloured lights, streamers, Union Jacks and the Stars and Stripes.

There are two silver bands. The Co-op and Hodgkiss - Willerbys.

They fiddle with their instruments, tap their feet, blow down and lubricate their mouthpieces. They slide off in ones and twos to the side door of the Bank Street Tavern for a gill – and they wait.

The Lady Mayoress, chain dangling, nods, waves, has a little word – and waits. The lads from the club wait too, lined up on one side of the little platform with the scouts, boy's brigade, girl-guides. The police are there, women's voluntary services, Saint John's Ambulance, quite a few dogs and some old soldiers with their berets and medals on.

'American General Visits Town.' The headline went.

'Come to tell us how they won the war.' Norman, Pat's friend tells them.

'Shagging all the women and shoving the prices up all over.'

And the rain, as it always does when you most wish it wouldn't – pisses down.

The sound of the roar of the out-riders comes first, giving the bands time to get back in their places, straighten their caps, adjust music stands.

The Mayoress and her retinue rise to the alert on the purple-clothed stage.

The cavalcade turns into the street with a precision that takes Patrick's breath away. The noise is incredible. Both bands striking up with what sounds more like a jazz tune than a military march. There is a throaty growl of Harley Davidson's, seven of them Pat counts, one out in front and three either side of the long, khaki, open-topped Buick. Shiny bright chrome sparkles on the bikes and the riders, white gloved, are tall, straight, erect in their saddles.

A roar goes up from the crowd gone mad with the sheer joy of it. They have seen nothing like this, ever. The dark war years, rationing. The blitz, austerity, their own natural reticence, fear of show – all are swamped, taken over by the pomp and unashamed confidence of this magnificent circus.

The general is a big man; stiff-backed. His olive-green helmet, close fitting, seems to be part of his great head. A few wisps of grey hair grow out of it at the sides and over the ears; four silver stars glint at his brow.

His chest carries row on row of medal ribbons, more stars. The legs are in jodhpurs and high, bright polished boots.

As he steps from the staff car, smiling, saluting, his spurs jangle on the carpeted steps of the platform. There is a holster at his hip, leather, deep tan to match his boots – a pearl-handled pistol nestles within. In all his young life, Patrick has never seen anything or anyone so grand, so beautiful.

I'll bet, he says to himself. This is what God looks like.

The general, still smiling, having been received by the Mayoress, rises before the hushed, expectant crowd.

He stands splay-legged, his eyes moving slowly over them. His cane tap tapping in a gnarled palm. Pat watches the general's eyes, trying to read what he is seeing. He sees – or Pat imagines he sees– pity. Suddenly, the eyes light up with a fire that seems to crackle on the air. The rain, as if commanded, has stopped.

The general turns to the little group of ex-servicemen.

'At ease men.' He begins, then, to them he says. 'I want to thank you for coming here today to greet me and, may I tell you that it makes me right proud to know that I belong to the same profession as your good selves.'

He has said exactly the right thing. The crowd goes wild again, hooting, clapping, cheering. The old men beam. Shoulders forced back in remembered discipline. The general holds up a hand. There is silence.

'And you – you young people;' the eyes Pat fancies, have fixed on his. He is talking to me, he thinks. It is as though he has been chosen, picked out, befriended and, in that moment Patrick would do anything the general commanded. The general goes on.

'This old world – as you have good reason to know – is in one holy hell of a mess. Well, I ain't here to tell you how to fix it. That is your job. The war is over. We done the fighting, me and my comrades here,' and he glances again at the veterans, by now fairly bristling with pride.

'All I can tell you is – start fresh. Do good. And always remember that for every great endeavour there has to be a first step.'

Well – Pat is in a dream after that. He feels lifted, sure. In that moment he seems to know that, no matter what the indications are to the contrary, the course of his life will change. Something will happen and when it does, all Pat has to do is recognise it and act. He walks homeward, through the wet, miserable, familiar streets. Patrons are lined up outside the Carlton cinema. 'Cont. Perfs.' The sign says – 'Continuous Performances, which means that a steady stream go in at about the same rate at which another stream comes out; hope briefly renewed, dreams refreshed, life made once more tolerable. They head for the chip shop and home.

Pictures. Thinks Patrick. Pubs. Umpteen churches and the mills, warehouses, coal tips, shunting yards. All these people for all those years. Labouring their guts out for a couple of hours of 'Gone With the Wind.' threepen'orth of chips and a lie in on a Sunday.

Patrick stops at the top of Gladstone Street. Turns and looks back at the town. His town. It lies, cupped in its bowl, glittering and false in its new, post-war orange lighting. The Pennine hills – ten minutes away by bus, loom, surrounding the town on three of its sides and, in the gap to his right lies Wales. Ireland and the great wide sea. He can feel the pull, the irresistible attraction of that small, natural gap in the hills. 'Escape.' The heavens breathe and 'This way out.'

All over town the new neon lights, brighter still than the streetlights, blink on and off, spelling out their various and insistent extravagances.

'Capstan.' The biggest of them says. Pink and blue it flashes out its famous message, which the local kids, using the initial letters and their own irreverent invention, have translated into; 'Can A Prick Stand Twice A Night?'

The answer to which, reading backwards becomes 'Now And Then Some Pricks Are Capable.' As he reaches the corner where his house stands and where on any other night he would feel the dread, the fear of opening his own front door, he laughs suddenly, wildly, out loud and, head thrown back to the gaping skies, he yells as hard as he can go.

'I am a Prick and I am Capable.'

Emily Entwhistle, engaged in her nightly task of putting out the cat and the milk bottles, looks up in shock at the sound of him.

'You tell 'em cock,' she says and her smile warms Pat as he goes in.

PIGGY

● ● ● ● ● ● ● ● ● ● ● ● ●

When you are very, very hungry and your stomach
thinks your throat is split, smells come in handy. They
fill you up - but only momentarily - then you have to have
another sniff. Seeing as I lived in a town that rejoiced
in smells I was laughing, never short of a quick pong.
There were cotton mills all over, dozens within easy
reach, giving off hot odours of oil, bleaching materials,
coke from the furnaces and a downpour, tangy, rich
in poisons, of fine rain filled with smoke from the tall
chimneys. We all had our favourite smell – Roocroft's
toffee works was high on the list. Maggee Marshall's

brewery. The Tannery. Mine was the Middlebrook. The river that meandered through most of the town, picking up, as it flowed, just about every ounce of effluent going. It was a colourful cocktail of discarded chemicals, dead dogs, busted bikes and used French letters. The whole thing steamed. You would pay a fortune for these waters at a fancy spa.

Colour was important. You had to watch it, the water, so that you could judge when the consistency was just right. Too much bleach for instance and you would rot your goolies off.

There was another famous way of loosing your goolies too – lads, and not a few girls (although they of course had less dangling, less to lose than the boys,) came from miles around to test their nerve against The Piggy.

A section of the Middlebrook flowed through Bobby Legs Park where a sluice had been fitted in years long gone by – probably to drive a water-mill – it was a long, gently sloping waterfall affair, covered in a slimy green growth, soft and as welcoming as thistledown. The water here was hot and a deep khaki in colour. In the centre, just where the stream tumbled over the sluice and into the main stream – was a hook, a metal projection, the remains no doubt of an iron railing that passed that way once. It was about five inches long, as thick as a man's thumb, bent viciously in the opposite direction to the river's flow – and with a point on it like a rapier. The idea was to slide down the sluice on your arse, bare-naked and – hopefully – miss the Piggy. Crowds would gather in summer time. It was like some ancient Roman games. Adults – who had done it themselves when young – would make clucking noises, shaking their heads, the while waiting and hoping for some poor soul to become snagged. Then there would be screams and blood and an ambulance called while the kid thus injured would be carted off to the Royal Infirmary to have everything stitched back on – or up. But it never happened. Never in living memory had anyone got caught. We lived in hopes and meanwhile, every-time you did it, got through safely, the thrill of having once more survived, defied the odds; coursed through your veins, sweet and powerful like a strong drink.

There were many of these testing grounds, trials to undergo. They did not make a lot of sense when you examined them coldly. But then, two world wars had just been fought in the space of less than thirty years

– there was not a lot we could do that would have been more stupid than that.

'The Spikes,' was yet another of these death defying stunts. Again it concerned the Middlebrook. The main river had several tributaries, some of them natural, many man-made. The Croal was one of these, a stinking channel, made of cobblestones, about two feet wide and criss-crossed by bridges, tunnels and pipes. One of these last, carrying steam from one part of a factory to another, was about ten inches in diameter, steel and with a long, menacing row of upward-pointing spikes running the full length of it. These of course were meant to stop kids using the pipe as a bridge. In fact a perfectly good bridge ran right alongside it. No self-respecting child however would deign to use it when such an attractive alternative was available.

'Going over the Spike,' the game was called and it was a scary business; feet splayed outward, shuffling along, the razor sharp, rusted barbs directly beneath ones tender parts. I confess it put the fear of God into me and I only ever did it for perhaps the same reason as most everybody else – I was too scared not to.

One day we were waiting for some younger lads to traverse the pipe. Egging them on, deriding the fainthearted, when suddenly, one of them. Little Johnny Mawdsley, about ten years old, slipped and fell, right down hard on the spikes. You never heard such a scream as went up from the poor kid.

'Maaam!' He yelled as the blood poured down, mixing and swirling in the muck of the water beneath. He was nearest to me and only one step away from the bank so, reaching out, I took hold of him and tried to lift him up. He came free easily - he must have only weighed about three stone – and I was all set to hoist him towards me and onto the bank, but there was a problem. The more I lifted him, the more he bled. What appeared to be gallons of blood gushed from his wounds, washing over the spikes, and the steel pipe. So I reversed the procedure. I pushed down. And the bleeding eased, almost stopped. He fought to release himself. 'Keep still you little bugger.' I yelled to no avail. The others, the onlookers, yelled too.

'Get off him. Let him go.' One of them grabbed me from behind, tried to pull me off. But I hung on, knowing an ambulance had been called. It was only a matter of time. And that is how they found me – the police and the ambulance men.

'Little bastard,' one copper said. 'He's trying to murder him,' and he gave me a clout alongside the ear.

Now that the ambulance men had the boy I collapsed, fell backwards, exhausted onto the bank. The police took me home, much against the wishes of the crowd who, if they had had their way, would have lynched me.

The coppers told my mother they would be around to collect me later.

And: 'Now you've done it,' my mother said. 'Mad bugger. I always knew you'd end up in jail. Just like your father you are.'

I tried to say, to tell them but nobody would let me.

'Bloody murderer – what harm did he ever do to you?' Is all I got.

The police came and took me to the infirmary for a check-up. Left me sitting, alone, in a corner of the waiting room while they muttered amongst themselves, discussing my crime. One of them, a sergeant, kept making pushing down movements and pointing at me. Finally, the doctor came over. He had a carnation in his buttonhole and a nice pinstriped suit. He clenched one of those single spectacles into one eye.

'So this is our little hero,' he said 'who taught you first aid? was it at school?' I was dumbfounded. I mean, I knew that what I had done had been the right thing but who was I against that lot?

They reckoned that my action in staunching the flow had saved Jimmy's last couple of pints and that if I had not done what I did the boy would have been dead when the ambulance came.

Well. What a turn around that was. Got my name in the paper, little hero. My old man bragging all over to anyone who would listen. Mother all moist eyed. 'Why didn't he say?' She kept on – 'Shy, that's what it is.' And she gave me a big hug for the cameras.

I see the lad every now and again. 'Blood brother,' he calls me, which has a nice ring to it.

PLATE PIES

● ● ● ● ● ● ● ● ● ● ● ●

'You can have your shilling, a tanner apiece, only you'll take that plate pie to your granny.'

That's what she was like Mrs. Laidlaw, Tommy's mam. Give you her right arm she would and then beat you over the head with the bloody stump for the rest of your life to remind you. There was always a catch, a forfeit to pay.

'Oh! Mam.' Tom protested. 'We'll miss the match – kick-off's at half past two.' Now even I did not think much to that for an argument. It was only just gone half past ten and Tom's gran' lived less than five minutes away even if you walked backwards, which we sometimes did for a bit of a change or to avoid bad luck. I knew his reasons of course – same as mine. Very funny, old folk, gave you the willies. Smothered in wintergreen ointment, pulling your cap down, getting your name wrong on purpose.

'Cough drops,' Tom said his granny smelt of, kissing him and – 'Mine's worse,' I told him. 'Milk stout and she sucks at your gob with no teeth in.' We both shuddered and vowed never to get old. Tom said that if he ever showed signs of it I was to shove him in't canal with a lead weight around his neck.

It was a funny thing, although neither of us considered it much at the time, but as far as we could see, we did not have a grandfather between us and, as for fathers, well, we had agreed early on Tom and me, that in the absence of any other evidence, both our dads were away fighting Germans in North Africa.

'Cop 'old of that.' Tom's mother commanded, handing him the wet end of a sheet and me the other.

'Make yourselves useful.' And of course that was another of her little tricks – going off the subject, catching you off balance, making you suffer.

Taking the folded sheets, she draped them on the clothes horse.

'Hoist that lot up our Billy,' she said and I did as I was told, pulleys squealing, waxed rope digging in on the palms of my hands.

'Right,' said Tommy, after much deliberation; consequences weighed up and in the realization that there was no way out.

'We'll get it took then.'

The pie. 'A nice meat and potato,' Mrs. Laidlaw said, was sitting on the kitchen table. A large, pink, spotted hanky enfolded it, with two big ears and a loop for carrying. Steam still whispered from the little slits in the golden brown crust. The smell was lovely. Brought tears to your eyes.

Tom's mam doled out the sixpenny pieces. Placing the coins, one at a time, first in my palm and then in Tommy's, folding our fingers over and then giving each hand a final squeeze.

'Stick tight,' she said, giving us a smile. As if we'd be likely to do otherwise. Still, we thanked her.

'Ta Mrs. L,' I said, whilst Tom wrestled with a big wet kiss and a hug that very nearly choked him.

Tom's gran was his mother's mother and she lived all alone in Threlfall Street. A single block of what had once been fine houses, with nice wide doorways and columns either side, peeling now for the want of a bit of paint. Neglected front gardens, busted windowpanes. Mill owners had kept them at one time; town dwellings. Now they were offices, a doss-house, back street bookies. One had a sign. 'Colonic Irrigation,' – which Tom said was something to do with overseas agriculture – and there was Miss. Joyce Timperley at number fourteen advertising Piano Forte. Deportment. Elocution – Hourly or By Arrangement.

I glanced at Tom as we went along, me rattling a stick in the railings and him with the pie in his hand. My best pal. My only pal, truth be known. Both fourteen and as people said; Alike as two peas in a pod or; Could have been twins. Straight blonde hair he had, with a bit stuck up in the middle. Chalk stripe trousers too big for him by about six months and a daft looking tie under a soft pale face. Actually, I'd always thought he looked a bit gormless which, seeing as I was his double, didn't say much for me.

It was in the basement, his gran's. Down some stone steps. Green moss at the edges. Rings on the flags where the milk bottles had been.

'Watch this,' said Tom, handing me the pie.

Bending low, he pushed open the flap of the letterbox with the tips of his fingers. 'Hey up Mrs. are you in?' He shouted. There was a silence.

He bang-banged hard on the panels of the door with a fist.

'Who is it?' came a voice. A cracked, dry, rustling voice with a cough in it.

'Who's there?'

'Why – it's me,' Tommy went.

'Yer fancy man – come to take you to the palais – get your frock on and let's get cracking.'

There was a pause, then.

'Ee! It's our Thomas.' Pleased.

'Here – wait a bit, just a minute.'

There came a crashing of bolts, a loud unlocking, another pause and then.

'Shove – you mun shove – only it sticks.'

So we shoved and the door creaked open.

The room, below ground level, windowless, was lit by a single gas lamp bracketed to one wall. There was no mantle, only the long, blue, hissing jet. There was a blackened spot above it, burnt into the ceiling. A narrow, scrubbed table stood at the centre, four wooden chairs arranged neatly around it.

There was a slop stone for a sink, brown earthenware, with a single cold-water tap on its snaky lead pipe, hovering above it. A small, low bed occupied one wall, quilted, and over that her clothes hung on nails driven into the plaster.

They were old clothes. Frocks from another age. A shawl, brocades and lots of black. In the centre, pride of place, wrapped in faded tissue paper – a wedding dress of yellowed ivory.

'What position are you playing gran?' Tommy asked, smiling, pointing to her legs which were clad in woollen football stockings, wrinkled, Wanderer's colours.

'You what,' she yelled, cupping one ear, bent almost double, polished clogs on tiny feet.

'Deaf.' Tom explained to me, pointing to his own ear. 'You'll have to shout.'

Her hair, swept back and tied in a bun, was silver but her eyes, the softest blue I had ever seen, were quick in a face so unlined, so fresh, it appeared to belong to somebody else; a girl's face, from long, long ago. My eyes went to the stockings again and I noticed bumps beneath the wool.

'Veins?' I asked Tommy.

'You what?' she said again. 'What does he say?'

'Very course veins,' Tom bellowed close to her ear. 'Have you got —?'

'Shallots.' She put in sharply. 'Little onions – against my sciatics.'

'Oh.' we both said and grinned.

'Sit you down,' She told us, busying herself at the knife drawer.

'I'll put that pie on to warm through.' My eyes had focused by now, grown used to the gloom and, looking around the tiny not untidy room, I suddenly saw the picture. Oval framed, sepia, dark with age, it hung from a rail on a time-blackened chain, facing, observing, the wedding dress opposite.

'Why. It's Uncle Harold,' I burst out.

We'd one just like it at home, in my granny's room. It was the same man, I was sure of it. The distinctive chin – lantern jaw they called it. Just like my own - and Tommy's. It ran in the male line and was considered handsome by them as didn't suffer from it. The uniform was the same, the swagger stick, even the armband – A lord Derby's man, my mother had told us. Kitchener's Army, killed at Gallipoli in nineteen fifteen.

Tom looked up, startled, following my gaze, as did the old woman who, though apparently not having heard my remarks had noted my interest in the picture. I felt her eyes flicker, to me, to Tom, to the picture again. Pausing, oven cloth in her hand, head screwed to one side, she continued to gaze then, turning, she went to fetch the pie from the oven.

'Your bellies will think that your throats are cut,' she said.

'Put them plates out our Tommy' – and, as she ladled out the steaming food, I caught her glancing once more at me, at Tom and at the soldier on the wall.

Wanderers lost – two nothing. It was a lousy game and my mind was not really on it anyway. I kept seeing that blooming photograph. One thing was for certain, Tommy's old gran had made me think and I didn't usually do a lot of that. I felt the penny beginning to drop on the way home just after we'd got past Moscrop's Cow Products down by the brewery. It's a powerful blend is that; hides stewing in the tannery, hops bubbling away next door. Clears the head.

The washing had dried by the time we got back to Tommy's house. His mother was doing the ironing. Pop – pop – pop the gas went, blue flame roaring. Crash! came the iron down hard, polishing and folding the hot stiffening sheets.

'That one,' Mrs. Laidlaw said, indicating yet another one of her pies, unwrapped, steaming on the sideboard, 'Is for Billy's mam and I dare say that her mother, partial as she is, will not say no to a slice.'

Tommy was getting the Bagatelle board out, rummaging about for the little steel balls, so I thought I would get one in quick.

'What's your mother's name Mrs.Laidlaw?' I asked, off hand like. 'Surname I mean?'

She looked at me for a bit. You know? like they do.

Then:

'Same as mine,' she said, 'what do you think? and if you're intending of playing with that,' she glanced at the Bagatelle, 'you can do it upstairs – and you can take these sheets up while you are at it.'

Now it is a fact that Tom and me looked alike but not only that, we sometimes thought the same thoughts. I could tell he had cottoned on when, piled high with sheets at the bottom of the stairs, he said to his mother;

'You know that photo mam? The soldier on gran's wall? Well, Billy's granny has one just like it.'

His mother said nothing for a bit then;

'well,' she said. 'it looks to me that little pigs have got big eyes as well as big ears – next thing you'll be telling us is that there's ponies down't pits. Take that pie on your way out.' Looking at me. A bit cold I thought.

We were both on leave last time we met, Tom and me. National Service, me in the navy and him a marine. We had a pint or two in The Grapes. We didn't stay long, both of us courting so we had to watch the pennies.

Next thing I heard, he'd been killed in Malaya. Ambush. Twenty years old he would be at the time. Not long after that my Grandmother went too. We buried her in Tonge cemetery and it poured down. There was me and my mother, one or two others. Mrs. Laidlaw came with her mother, Tom's granny, looking very feeble.

She came up to us after and she says:

'Touch your collar for luck sailor boy?'

Then, turning and squinting up at me:

'He favours,' she said, 'don't he? around the eyes – that lovely chin?'

SUCKED

●●●●●●●●●●●●●

'Shift your feet, place is like a tip.' Ada Moscrop is a large woman, gets her frocks mail order, outsize, in which she looks as feminine as a barrel of lard in a tent. She constantly scrubs things, Ada. Beats carpets with no mercy. When she is not immersed in suds she'll be wringing or wiping, grim-faced, determined in the pursuit of dirt.

Henry, her husband, is mouse-like and fits, being male, into that same category which includes all things unclean. Liable,unless kept drenched in deodorant, to stink. She has all the modern amenities – a washing machine, automatic and with a sanitising cycle normally found only in hospital sterilising departments. There is a dishwasher of course and a vacuum cleaner, always a vacuum cleaner. It is the latest in a long line of such implements having had its beginnings twenty five years back when they were first married with an upright, next a cylindrical, followed by an orbital and now, the very acme of suction cleaners, the dual, all-purpose microbotic – Ada's dream machine.

'Sucks anything,' the salesman told them. 'Wet or dry; built in centrifuge where solids and liquids are separated and of course, a garbage disposal unit fitted as standard.'

Henry, generally sceptical of the claims of door to door salesmen, had been impressed. Not that it made any difference; his opinion had not been sought. Nonetheless he had liked the looks of it.

He was a bit of an inventor, Henry. In a modest way of course; folding coat hangers, a device to fumigate the canary, that sort of thing. Upon reading the instruction manual he had been intrigued by the specifications: Tank capacities: Dry: Nought point five cubic metres. Wet: Fifty litres. Rate of Centrifuge: Six thousand five hundred revs. per min. Very interesting. And the suction on it. Twenty nine point nine inches of vacuum. That was very nearly perfect. Henry knew a thing or two about vacuum. How nature would try to destroy it. How, if it were possible to reach absolute zero in temperature – something like minus two hundred and seventy degrees centigrade – a complete void could be achieved and, this was the bit that thrilled Henry; at this point the whole world, possibly the universe, would collapse into a big, black, bottomless hole.

Feet carpet-slippered, legs held high in an attitude of complete and abject submission, Henry strove desperately for dignity whilst Ada, plunging and scavenging, stripped bare the already clean area around him. It was then that the idea came to him. The thought. So blindingly simple, so apt as to be almost comical. He winced at the thrill of it and a spasm, a grimace gripped his face in a foxy smile. Ada switched off the din.

'What's the matter with you?' she enquired, her tone a challenge. 'Wind? well you can think again. Get some salts down you and go for a walk.'

Up on the heath he strolled and pondered. He was surprised, even a little shocked to find that, once accepted, how easy, how right the concept became. He ticked off a few parameters in his head as he walked, looking as he did so for all the world like your average middle aged man wondering what to do about the black fly on his roses.

Ada's mass equalled two hundred and fifty pounds of which, or so he believed, ninety per cent was water. Some research was required here but roughly what did we have? Let's see: One pound avoirdupois is what? Zero point four six kilograms? About that. So; two fifty pounds equals one one five kilograms of which only a tenth is hard stuff – bone, finger nails and so on – which is eleven point five kg. Not a lot He was quite surprised, anyway, say fifteen kilo's of solids, some of which, the larger pieces – tibia, fibula, pelvic girdle etcetera would need reducing, breaking up. He imagined that, once she was sucked dry, a few smart whacks with a sledge hammer would do the trick very nicely. He'd had a quick look at the gadgets; various brushes, nozzles and tubes and it seemed to him that, with a bit of arrangement and modification, the piece designed for carpet shampooing would be ideal. By stretching Ada's considerable mouth and knocking out her few remaining teeth, the attachment would, with some persuasion, fit nicely. Any gaps would have to be sealed off. He rather thought a good epoxy resin might be the thing here. All other orifices would have to be plugged. A horrid thought but still, if you want to make an omelette.......

It would perhaps be as well to leave one hole adjustable, yes that might be best, to allow air ingress and thus prevent the carcass from collapsing prematurely and before all the liquids had been extracted. It would have to be a bung he decided. One of the kind used in pubs to broach a barrel. It would provide just the right rate of flow and he rather thought you could get the self tapping type which made its own thread as you screwed it in. Now, what else? Oh. Yes: He could hardly expect Ada to remain still, mouth wide open, while he knocked her teeth out and as for the other indignities, no, something would have to be done to immobilise her. A clout on the head? Too crude and in any case she'd be likely to clout him back and that would be the end of it – and him too probably. Asphyxiation, that was the ticket, delivered in a puff from one of her own aerosols; chloroform or ether, one of those would do it and leave him free to fix her up.

He had started on his way home. Dusk was coming on, a lovely warm evening in late July. A small boy, his hand shading his face from the setting sun, watched as his kite bobbed, weaved and soared in the red-streaked sky. That's the way, Henry thought. Freedom. Boy and kite, utterly free and he smiled contentedly as he went on his way.

Now Ada's concern for cleanliness extended far beyond the mere infrastructure of their home. It included a particular interest in Henry's insides. Tea, as per usual, was a light meal. One dry biscuit, half a banana and two cups, no more if you please, of very weak, sugarless tea. All other meals contained purgatives of one kind or another. Prunes, for instance at breakfast. Spinach or some other silage at lunch and, for their supper, going-to-bed meal, hot chocolate laced with a spoonful of senna pods. Henry was very regular.

He sat now sipping his tea, observing her over the rim of his cup. It had been established long since that, being a woman, she had no need, except very occasionally, for any help in her natural functions and this fact, coupled with a voracious appetite allowed her to eat like a pig. He watched her now, shovelling it down and the resentment arose like bile in the pit of his ravaged stomach. Soon, he mused. Oh. How I will eat. Pork chops and sausages. Raw beef on toast. Oh the things I will get up too. Smoking my head off, kicking the cat, telling rude jokes down at the pub.

His habit, encouraged by Ada to get him out of her way, was to retire after tea to his shed at the bottom of the garden where he had his 'playthings,' as she called his precision tool set, his lathe and modelling bench – all the paraphernalia of the dedicated, if restricted, handy-man.

Settled at his bench he soon had it all down on paper, slide rule computations checked and re-checked, a working drawing in third angle projection and, as a final touch, a critical path analysis of the whole enterprise. He nodded, smiled, settled back in his chair. Very good. He said out loud. Very good indeed. Then, knocking out the dottle from his once – a - day - only pipe, he arose, stretched, switched off the light and, with only a very faint murmur in protest, dropped dead.

'Never knew what hit him,' their GP. told her cheerfully. 'Lovely way to go – if you have to. Heart of course. You can never tell at that age.'

Ada was distraught. How was she going to manage? They'd chop his pension sure as eggs, lucky if she got a third. It was not fair after all she had sacrificed. Just like him it was and she would sob, pale behind her veil, the very picture of the grieving widow. Her brother George came down to help with the rituals, things to be done. Cremation was the best thing they both thought. Henry would have wanted it and it was as Ada said, cleaner.

It shocked her to discover that they burnt the coffin. Such a waste. You'd have thought a bit back on the empty but no, up it went and Henry with it. She was glad she'd had a look just before they secured the lid. Neat as a pin he was. Shoes could have done with a rub but still – and she had contented herself with a quick flick with her handkerchief at a speck of dust on his moustache, then she stepped back and with a small dry yelp, fainted quite successfully as they banged him up.

Life went on of course, she would not after all, be destitute, he had left her a little. Insurance and so on, what remained of his pension. Life would be at the very least, tidy.

One day, some seven or eight weeks later, George called. He had been looking through Henry's bibs and bobs, the stuff in the shed and it looked as though she might be on to a bit of alright.

'That last thing he was working on?' George said. 'Well, I showed it to a mate of mine down at the club, he's rather a boffin himself and he reckons it could be just what they are looking for – chicken factories you know? – processing? He says he sees no reason why abattoirs won't jump at it, pathology labs, mortuaries – no end to it.'

And there wasn't. Apparently Henry's brainwave had included features not previously articulated and, while it was true that his idea had not progressed beyond the drawing board stage, that idea, with prudent marketing, could make her a fortune. And it did. Very quickly. In the space of a year she had given up the bungalow and taken residence in a rambling old manse in the Lake District. She'd a staff of some five retainers – the majority in a sanitary capacity – working under her supervision. There was hardly a minute in any one day when, somewhere in the labyrinth of corridors, bedrooms, kitchens, there was not some aspect of cleaning going on.

Her chauffeur, green-liveried, twenty six, handsome, was a Spaniard and, to the eye of even the most casual observer, it may have been supposed that his employment had somewhat more to it than the mere driving of a motor car. Once a fortnight she would visit the cemetery and, as a self imposed task, perhaps a penance which she vowed to continue as long as she lived, she took along a small hamper of cleaning materials. It had been one of Henry's little notions, a compact container with pockets and pouches wherein all manner of scrubbing brushes, scouring pads, soaps and strong sprays could be carried with comfort from job to job.

Henry's remains had been placed, at Ada's request, on a hard standing of concrete. Away from trees and the nuisance of leaves and close to a water tap where she could brew up her suds. George had arranged, again at her request, for a small hole to be drilled in the lid of Henry's urn and her final act, on each visit, after a thorough skirmish of the area, a good sluice down and a polish, was to take out the little plug and give four short squirts of deodorant straight into the heart of Henry's ashes.

'It is the least,' she would say with a heavy sigh. 'The very least I can do.'

THE LESSON

●●●●●●●●●●●●●

Patrick James Delaney had read somewhere that life was nothing more than a series of lessons. They happened constantly. You either learned from them or you did not. He supposed that God had something to do with it. Whoever He was. Anyway, Pat kept a good eye open for lessons and, though most of the time the ones that came his way were so vague as to be almost invisible, every now and again one would come along that was so obviously an instruction, you would have to be blind as a bat not to see it. Or feel it. As was the case with Finney the Haddock.

Finney, otherwise known as Ronnie Riley, was a strange boy and he arrived in an equally strange way. Usually, any addition to a family came about in a recognised manner. It was only natural. A woman would be seen to have put weight on. She would stop, resting at the street corner, a hand at the small of her back. Telling the neighbouring women:

'By heck, he's giving me some gyp, little bugger.' They would tell her that the swelling in her legs had gone down; they would go on about carrying. Recite some horror stories concerning their own last do - and that would be that, you would know. A baby was due. This fellow – Ronnie – came all at once, aged twelve, on the train from down South. One minute there was old Mister and Missus Riley, number eight they lived at - front step always nice, church on a Sunday, then there was him, turning up like that, as large as life. With a tie on.

Son, they called him but;

'He's no son,' was what the others said. 'Why, she's sixty-two if she's a day and him? Well look at him. Only got one leg.' It was true. Angus Riley's other leg was pot. Pink. He had shown it to us once and told how he had buried the real one with full military honours some while back at Suvla in Turkey.

It was thought at first that Ronnie had jaundice, there was a lot of it about but it turned out to be suntan so Pat gave him a good hiding for showing off. It was Patrick who named Finney not long after he first arrived. Always fishing, the newcomer was. On his own in the lodge by Ramsay's Bleach Works and though no haddock were to be found there, it seemed a good enough name, raised a few laughs, especially when you considered the colouring.

It was policy in those days to dislike new things or strangers, just in case. You could always change your mind later on if you felt like it. Of course Pat went a bit further than that with Ronnie. Perhaps it was the success over the naming, perhaps Ronnie's smallness.

He was littler than Pat and there were not so many as were so Pat picked on him. He was sorry about it in his heart of hearts, for he knew what it was like. He had some to put up with at home and in any case he liked Mister Riley, one leg or not and he had wished that he were his own dad instead of the one that he had who, when he wasn't bashing folk, grunted.

Everywhere, for the best part of a year, Patrick baited the lad. The suntan soon went and Finney was quite pale underneath, sickly in fact and he was often absent from school. Pat would catch him doing an errand and if any of the lads were about he would go over and clout him one. The boys would all jeer and Finney would run off.

'Get to your mam.' They would yell and he would obey, shoulders stooped, bleating like a lost lamb.

One day Mister Riley stopped Patrick on the street at the corner by Hampsons bakery. Pat thought he was in for a telling off, a warning. It was not like that at all. What the man said was, had Patrick thought of joining the Lad's club?

'Our Ronnie's started going,' he told him. 'Doing very well, gymnastics, weight lifting, that sort of thing.' And off he went, saying good evening and lifting his cap like he always did.

Spring came. The weather changed and street games with it. Lads got out their bats and balls, their marbles. Girls started pushing prams about, hushing and cooing over other folk's babies and Ronnie, slowly at first but then with ever increasing confidence, altered. Patrick noticed that punches, aimed at his victim's head, somehow fell short. A sure-fire belt to the belly connected not with soft flesh but with fresh air, making Pat stumble, nearly fall flat and to wonder if his arms had shrunk. He called Ronnie a sissy for not standing still and 'Just you wait,' he told him. Next time he would knock his blooming block off and then he went home for a bit of a think and his tea. Pat had very good reasons for wanting to stay on top of his adversary. Apart from the praises heaped upon him by his mates the lads. There was the attitude of his own father. Patrick had observed that, ever since the vendetta started, Mister Delaney's interest in his son had undergone a change. He would boast to neighbours: 'That's my lad that. A chip off the old block.' And 'Make a man of him yet.'

Now, while it was true that Pat had no wish to be a chip, nor even a splinter of that particular block, dislike of Ronnie being more like affection compared to his feeling for his own father; still, the manliness angle appealed, so he pursued it blindly, seduced by his own significance and the promise of new found stature. Suddenly, it was summer. Holiday time. Tar melted in the nicks between the cobbles. Streets, hushed by shut down mills, stewed in the heat and Patrick, fancying himself as Joe Louis; Rocky Marciano; Field Marshall

Mont- bloody- gomery and all; in one belligerent ball, over one half hour on a glorious September day, learned for the first but not for the last time that life, jolly as it can seem to be on occasion, every so often and without so much as a postcard for a warning, erupts with a vehemence so awful you wish you had stayed home and read comics.

Ronnie was on his way to bible class. Sunday best suit on. Nice polished shoes. Waltzing along in the middle of the road. Unusual that. Pat should have been warned. There he was: Finney the Haddock, more brass than a bloody tomcat. Asking for it.

Queen street mission stood at the entrance to the little park. They could hear hymns being sung. A fair crowd had gathered, word having gone around from street to street of back-to-back houses. There was a scrap on.

Small boys and some not so small. One or two girls, out they all came, a couple of dozen of them. Expectant, anxious not to miss the first blow. Longing for tears and some blood. Organ music swelled, rising, rich and powerful, bursting into the open air as both mission doors were suddenly opened.

Finney Haddock came out last. He smiled, glancing once towards the waiting crowd. He shook hands with one or two of his fellow worshippers, handing over his bible to one of them, presumably for safekeeping. He smiled again.'Ta, ra.' He said and set off.

'He's going to the Mop end.' A shrill voice piped.

It was true. Finney, apparently scorning the comparative safe passage afforded by the main road, had taken the long, dangerous route. It was a well-known fact and you would have to be new to the area or very stupid not to know it; when it came to The Mop you went mob handed. Predatory gangs skulked among its many dark by-ways and it was said, vouched for as gospel by more than one envied witness, that dirty old men could often be seen there, lurking about with no clothes on. Here was Finney the Fearless Haddock taking a stroll as if he owned the blooming place.

It was then that Patrick sensed that something was going terribly wrong. He was, without a doubt, in for it.

Finney had stopped; his jacket, which he had already removed, hung on the branch of a nearby tree. He was still smiling. 'Hello Pat.' He said pleasantly.

Patrick, having given up on the hope of a sudden kindly heart attack, resigned to his fate, was relieved of any kind of reply, even if he had known what to say, by the hot, urgent cries of the crowd.

'Cock him. Cock him. Cock him.' They brayed, pushing Pat forward eagerly, anxious to get the job started.

A slight, pretty girl, known for her painful shyness, pushed her little face full into that of Patrick, eyes wide, spit flying, she mouthed a big 'O' and screamed, 'Kill him Pat,' and 'Murder.'

The ritual began. Placing a finger on each of their chests in turn, first his opponent's and then his own, Patrick chanted the ages old challenge.

'One two three, I'm cock o' thee. If tha touches me, I'll touch thee.'

Then, heart hammering fiercely, left fist ready, he made the first move. 'Touched thee.' Silence. Nobody stirred. Then, from Ronnie, 'Touched thee back,' as his small bony fist came down like an axe on Patrick's ribs.

The pain was electric, stunning and sharp. Patrick turned, crouching, gasping, sudden tears blinding him. He rubbed his eyes and there was Finney, in classic boxer's pose. Head hunched down into his protecting shoulder, chin well in behind the waiting left fist, right arm outstretched. He pivoted Pat like a kite on a string and the right fist came down again, agonisingly, in precisely the same spot, under the ribs and the kidneys.

Again and again the blows came. The crowd yelling blue murder.

'Kill him Finney.' The cry now went and Patrick was down, bent on one knee, sobs bursting from his pain - stretched lips as Finney the Haddock, his own tears free now, lowered his arms.

He stood, chest heaving, remorse creasing his face, looking down at what he had done. Then, turning on his heel, he took up his jacket and draped it gently around Pat's thin shoulders. The on-lookers, strangely silent now, disturbed by something outside their ken, broke ranks, began to drift away in ones and twos, their eyes averted.

The small girl, eyes still wild, lingered. She stared un-blinking down at the pair. Then, losing interest, she tossed two worn tennis balls into the air and began to sing.

'One, two, three, allura. Four, five, six, allura.'

The balls rose and fell in a regular rhythm as, with a tight, fixed smile on her pinched, hungry face, she wandered away, without looking back, to join the others.

THE REVENGE OF EPHRAIM YATES

●●●●●●●●●●●●●

He dabbed the styptic pencil where he had cut himself shaving, wincing at the sting. Getting old, that's what it boiled down to. Old and nearly useless. Fancy, reduced to knocker-up at the railway sheds. Him. Head trimmer, thirty five years down the pit and laid off at sixty. Silicosis. Some thanks.

There was the pension of course – industrial injury – he managed alright, saved a bit, did his shopping on a pay day. Kept the house clean. Not so neat as Doris of course. He had always wanted to go first. Selfish but there it was. Things could be worse. But that lad Alec. Only sixteen and God. Ephraim swore he was evil. What had he ever done to the boy? Got old he supposed.

The kid seemed to hate him, always coming out with remarks, getting up to tricks. Dangerous that's what he was. Why, Ephraim had almost lost his job over that joke Alec had played a week or so back, the very first night Ephraim had gone out knocking on his own. Two rows of identical railwaymen's cottages, back to backs. All sorts living in them now, since the cut-backs. Alec had swapped all the blooming gates around, leaving Ephraim, unknowing, banging away at all the wrong houses. Frightened the day-lights out of one old dear.

'I'm on my own here,' she'd cried, teeth in a jar somewhere, hair in curlers. Stupidly he had replied:

'Well, according to this list, you've the six-fifteen light engine to Patricroft.'

That had got around quick, he'd never live it down. Worse was when he had knocked at what was supposed to be twelve Mallard Avenue and which turned out to be fourteen Flying Scot Place. Naturally the man – on the dole as it happens – had been upset, getting woken up half way through the night but – setting an Alsatian dog onto him? He felt so impotent, there was no reasoning with the boy and it was making life a misery.

Later, over a pint with Albert he had spilt it all out. His friend was the only one he could have told. They were pals. Schoolmates first, then El Alemein with the Fusiliers. He had never known a time when there was no Albert; grave-digger now, part time, since his heart attack.

'Beats the mill though, out in the fresh air, not cooped up going yellow with no light in the snuffy.' Always carefree, cheerful, Albert.

'What about we put the wind up the young beggar?' he'd said.

'How?' queried Ephriam.

'This-wise,' his friend had replied: 'You know we are on overtime at the cemetery, flu epidemic like? Well, you know that on one of your rounds knocking up, you take a short cut through St. Jude's? I've often thought, in the middle of the night, that if I were to pop up from my hole, out from behind one of them big angels say, to ask a passer-by the time, well, some people might get quite a nasty turn out of something like that. Do you follow Eph.?'

'I do,' said Ephraim warmly. 'Friday morning, two-thirty, we'll be coming through from Ainsworth Lane end.'

'Right,' said Albert.

'Sup up,' said Ephraim. 'We'll have another.'

By the time Ephraim had set off for the sheds next day, his natural inoffensive nature re-asserting itself, he had begun to have second thoughts. A joke was a joke. This could turn out to be a pantomime. However, ten minutes in the company of Alec in the mess-room after clocking on, was enough. The lad had had one or two drinks by the look of things and he was even more abusive than ever in that sly, digging way of his.

'You're looking well old cock – have you been ill? you'd better get your skates on tonight instead of them clogs. Old folk. Smelling of winter green, should be in a home.'

As usual, once they had set off on the round. Ephraim with the lamp and Alec clutching the list of calls, not a word passed between them. Ephraim knew that the insults were only meant for work-mates ears. It was all bravado. Still it hurt nonetheless. It hurt a lot.

They had one more knock at the bottom of the lane, before turning into the grave-yard: Tommy Partington: Four fifteen fish out of Moses Gate.

'Righto,' called Tom as his light snapped on. 'Tha needn't knock bloody door down,' and they were off, round the corner and in, through the big, black, iron gates.

It was a cold night, frost before day-light likely. A half moon and a mist that seemed to seep up out of the stone path in front of them, hanging, curling about the bushes. Night sounds, distant, amplified on the still air came, clear and recognisable. The deep hoarse cough of a Stanier 5MT as she laboured up Chequerbent Bank. The tap-tap-tapping of a shunter, shrill with her whistle as she hit the trucks up. Ephraim stamped his clog irons on the ringing flag-stones. Partly to warn Albert, partly for comfort. He swung his oil lamp, casting slants of light through the fog, among the headstones and statues. Here a large soot blackened angel, arms and wings outstretched. There the stern, censorious bust of some long departed mill owner.

'It is a mournful place,' muttered Ephraim, 'and I know what's coming.'

Suddenly, from beside the piled up earth of a new dug grave; floating, feet lost in the clinging ground mist, full in the beam of Ephraim's lamp; the apparition arose, a long, pointing finger stretched before it. Even Ephraim gave a start.

'By the gum,' Albert, You've done us proud.' Obviously his pal had taken more care over his role than he had let on at their earlier discussion. He was dressed for the part. Foot-plate gear he had on; shiny-topped peaked cap, bib and brace overalls buttoned once at the neck, a silver watch-chain across his belly. Even a twist of cotton waste sticking out of a trouser pocket.

'By the Norah,' muttered Ephraim. 'Tha should be on't stage.' Now for his own part: Stepping fearlessly up close to the beckoning sight, he raised an admonishing finger:

'Get thee gone spectre. Get back in thy hole and shut up.' Out of the corner of his eye he glimpsed Alec. The lad was stopped, frozen in mid-stride, mouth agape, one hand palm out as if to ward off the awful apparition that had so abruptly appeared in front of him. All the cockiness gone. Struck dumb. Finally a cry croaked out of his quivering lips.

'Mam. Oh. Mam.' He turned, staggered and was off, boots beating wildly on the pavement, knocking up list flying in his wake, towards the cemetery gates.

'Hell,' exploded Ephraim. 'We've gone too far. I'd best be after him.' And, not pausing to thank Albert for his performance, he ran as fast as his one lung would let him, down the path to Ainsworth Lane and the sheds.

'Well,' said the shift foreman as Ephraim, panting, opened the mess-room door. 'I don't know what you've been up to – I've had to send that lad home, couldn't get a word out of him save he wanted his mother. Is he sickening for something or what?'

'He left sudden,' said Ephraim guiltily. 'Happen he's eaten something.'

He passed the rest of his shift quietly, sweeping between the wheels of the softly steaming, banked engines, worried. It had been a bit over the top. He sincerely hoped that the lad would be alright in the morning.

Back home, washed at the sink, a pot of tea before him, Ephraim, hardly having slept for wondering about Alec, was trying to read his paper when rat-a-tat-tat at the front door and there looking well, composed if a bit sheepish, stood the very lad.

'Hello Mister Yates' - Mister, that made a change – it was usually Effy or Moses or whatever your flaming name is. 'I thought I'd pop round, see if you are alright like, only, it's funny how imagination plays you tricks.' Then in a rush: 'Best not say owt about last night Eh Mister Yates? Only, well, you know what they are like at the sheds. That grass needs cutting I see.' Nodding down at the tiny strip of lawn in Ephraim's palisade. 'Shall I come round after the ten-till-six and give it a trim?'

'Aye lad,' smiled Ephraim. 'And if tha says nowt then nowt'll be said.' The boy flushed his pleasure. 'Ta. Mister Yates – see you on shift.'

Ephraim sat. 'Well I don't know – turned out alright I suppose.' He chuckled recalling the lad's relief. 'Just a kid, that's all. Just an ordinary pleasant lad under all that.'

The door knocker went again, quick, angry, startling him from his thoughts. Rupert's eldest – Muriel he thought it was, a disapproving frown on her pinched, anxious face, stood agitating on the step.

'My dad's sent me round from the Infirmary – intensive care and all. Important he said it was – here,' – and she thrust a slip of paper into his hand.

Dear old pal. Ephraim read. Rushed in here sudden yesterday morning, ticker again. Not bad now and mending. Sorry I couldn't make it to St. Jude's this morning. Happen we'll set it up later. Yours truly, Albert.

HAPPIDROME

●●●●●●●●●●●●●

The stink was always the same, stale cabbage, various ointments, the vermin behind the wallpaper. Gas lit, the room had a neglected look. Piles of clothing waiting to be ironed, dozens of newspapers, a pram with bits of broken biscuits among the soiled bedding, broken toys. On the table top was the debris of long ago meals, dirty plates. Shiny black cockroaches rummaged, antennae waving wildly and, as Patrick turned up the jet, they fled, quick, furtive and with sickeningly soft thuds they hit the linoleum floor, skittering to the safety of dark corners.

'Oh. It's you,' said his mother, hunched, shawled in her chair by the fireside.

'Do you want some coal on that?' asked Pat in reply, nodding to the fire that had nearly gone out.

'Is there any?' she wondered absently. 'Only I missed him, the coal man, unless he's changed his day.' Unless you were still in bed more like, thought Pat wryly. Then: 'I'll have a look,' as he went out to the yard.

He wished he could be more civil to her, his mother. She had been lovely once or so everybody told him. Smart, lively.

'Cleanest house around,' they would say. 'That grate – why it were black leaded that often it were half an inch thick with it.' He looked at her now over the tea he had made; soiled pinny, strands of loose, greasy hair. Worn out.

'Do you want your teeth?' he asked, trying his best. They would be grinning in their jam jar; pink gummed, bubbles rising, on the shelf over the sink.

'Nay,' his mother said. 'I'm off up in a bit – you'd best be as well, it's his Buffs night.'

Drunk then, he would be, his father, full of mouth as usual. Re-telling what he had told them at the lodge, how he had put them straight: 'Grand master? Grand arsehole, more like.' He would start a row in a monastery, famous for it; a big, howling brute of a man with not a gentle consideration in his entire, unyielding body.

Why? Pat asked the question, silently and for the thousandth time. Why had she married him? He knew the answer of course – she had been five months gone with himself inside her, that was why and it explained a lot. He poked the embers to warm them both, breaking a cob of smouldering coal so that bright sparks danced among the flames, sending up blue-yellow spurts of flashing colour to the roaring of the damper as the fire drew. The long, iron poker, brass handled, glowed dull red; its tip deep in the maw of the blaze. The woman, nodding in her chair, hummed a snatch of song. She looked up at him, her slack toothless smile broadening.

'We three in Happidrome,' she began. 'Working for the BBC. Ramsbottom and Enoch and me.' She continued humming then; 'Happidrome.....' she spoke the word softly, a long, sobbing sigh that moved the boy, made him want to get up and go to her, hold her, say it would be alright, that he would......what? make it all go away? kiss it better? what could he do? He remained motionless, sipping his tea noisily to hide his hot tears.

Patrick knew that there were other, better ways of living. He had seen it in the homes of his friends. Everyone was in the same boat money-wise and yet some managed better and in a happier, more convivial way than his family. There was no love here, that was the main problem and yet 'To my Darling Wife,' the birthday cards said while his mother was nursing a split lip. Pat could never work it all out and he was tired of trying.

The door went – rat - tat – tat.

'Who's that?' asked his mother. 'At this time.'

'It's Billy,' came the answer, muffled through the door. 'Can you come out Pat?'

'Out?' said Patrick – 'why, it's gone nine - o – clock. What's going on?'

'Your Dad,' said Billy. 'and mine, down the shelter.'

He meant the air raid shelter at the end of the street. Dis-used now and abandoned two years after the end of the war. They'd happy memories of the shelter. Huddled there in the dark, enjoying the fear of the grown-ups. An adventure, that's what it had been. The Dornier 207's slow throbbing overhead, on their way to Salford docks where they had lit up the sky with their incendiaries. The crump and bang of high explosive bombs. Shaken earth filtering through the cement cracks. The smell of sweaty bodies, piss and candle-smoke.

'I saw them get off the bus and go down. What do you suppose...?'

They took off their boots as they went. Pat had a torch.

'Quiet,' he said and they went down the ramp leading to the black hole of the entrance.

The passageways were cold, winding, lined with three - tier bunks as they made their way downward. They came to a cross roads and stopped.

'Which way?' Bill mimed with raised shoulders when, suddenly there was a sound, a murmuring and they followed in the direction it had come from. They could see now the glow of a candle along the passage and they headed for it, stepping carefully to avoid giving the alarm.

They had reached the final wall and they could tell by the noises coming from the other side that, whatever it was that was going on, they were about to find out. They paused. Pat raised an eyebrow at Billy as they tried to make out the sounds: Harsh, laboured breathing, the slap – slap – slap of flesh on flesh and, suddenly and simultaneously they knew. Pat switched on his torch and stepped into the space ringed and lit by the flickering candle.

His eyes took in the scene before him. He became a camera, snapping and recording: His eyes met those of his father and locked, lingered before the two boys ran, tearing along the passageways, desperate to get out and into the cold night air.

'Best say nothing,' Billy said as Pat's mind, already racing with the possibilities, sought to grasp, to give credence to the sight he had just seen. How would he react, his father? A beating most likely, but, then?

Pat examined his own feelings and found, most surprisingly; compassion. He felt sorry; protective. He wished he could somehow undo what had happened. He remembered his father as he had been, years ago now in Pat's short life. Memories of a happy, wide-smiling man, jogging him on one knee. Folk songs, of which the man had known dozens, mainly Irish and stirring:

'When our Tommy joined the Territorial's, ours was a happy little home.' All the way back to his house Pat allowed himself to ruminate on what had once been, what was and, now, what was likely to be.

The next morning he had the house to himself. His mother, part time now at the mill where she had worked ever since a girl and his father nowhere to be seen. Pat was dreading their next meeting. They never spoke to each other in the normal course of a day, so that was no problem but what about the eyes – how could he ever look into those of his father ever again?

'What's it reading?' the man might enquire of Pat via his mother and that was one of their bones of contention, Pat read – and his father could not, except in a stumbling fashion, his lips moving to the words and a finger following the letters on the page. Pat realised, in his more receptive moods such as the one that gripped him now, that the man was nothing more nor less than a product of his own early environment. He too had been whipped and beaten as a boy; neglected, unloved and now he was doing the same to his own.

Pat remembered the man in uniform, high polished boots and swinging arms.

'Off to win the war for us, our Jimmy,' the neighbours all said as off he would go, striding down the street.

'To kill Germans,' he said when they questioned his going. 'Same as they killed our Harold and our George in the first lot.'

The army invalided him after they had patched him up, sent him home in hospital blue. Home to the disappointment, the dole queue and a house full of kids.

On the Monday morning following the affair in the air raid shelter Patrick awoke to the smell of bacon frying. His father often did this. The plates, loaded with the freshly fried food, would be laid out on the hearth in front of a blazing fire; crispy, lean bacon, pink-shaded fried eggs and a slice of toast. One plate for each of the family, still lying in their beds. All except Pat. He was left out, always.

But not this particular morning, there it was, Pat counted them and his mother, just out of bed, remarked upon it:

'Best get it down you – and no questions asked,' and Patrick did, with relish but not without a fair amount of what he identified as guilt. Why couldn't he acknowledge his father's obvious attempt at some sort of rapport? It was not the first time he had felt the older man trying. All Pat had to do surely was meet him part way. Saying a simple thanks for the breakfast would be a start. But he could not make that move; the gulf between them was too wide. He was confused and needed solace.

Patrick's attendance at church – which was just across the street – was never achieved on Sundays nor at any of the other recognised times. Neither did he frequent the church proper. His place of worship, if such it could be called, was the belfry and he made his way there now.

The stairway was cold, gritty to the touch, a stone spiral reaching from the little vestry, lined with the surplices of choir boys, white, slashed with scarlet, hanging on their hooks, as if in parody of the boys themselves. He felt a thrill as he always did on entering the cramped space. The musty smell of hymn books and dead flowers, the silence after the noises of the street. He made his way up, hanging on to the rope which acted as a hand rail.

Pigeons stirred as he approached; fluttered, startled and then settled down again into their ceaseless rhythms. The males, chests puffed out, strutting; arrogant for the females who were constantly at odds with these seemingly unwanted advances. And yet – yes, there they were, new since the last time he was here, two pure white eggs among the scratchings of the shit strewn floor, a rude beginning from which the fledglings would later escape and soar to the skies.

Patrick squatted by the louvered opening, the great, bronze bells at his back and the streets laid out below him. Line after line of back to back terraces, outside privies, the co-op on the corner and the yards of waving washing hung out to dry. Old man Foster was doing his rounds:

'Bone.' He cried. 'Donkey stone – rag bone,' as he rattled his cart on the cobbles. Pat was at peace here. He could see without being seen, secret, and it was the nearest he ever came to a feeling of content.

Millie the cat came forward to meet him as he approached the door of his house. Her tail twitched angrily as she rubbed her neck on the bricks of the wall. She mewed plaintively as she came.

'Been in a fight have we?' Pat asked and she rubbed his leg in reply.

The key, on its string, came free of the letter box and Pat opened the door.

He saw the shadow first, blotting out the sunshine which normally filled the hall way at this time of day. A pool of liquid; brown, muddy had formed on the bottom stair and it was replenished by a steady dripping emanating in tear-drop shapes from the toe of his father's left shoe. The other shoe was missing. Black marks scored the plaster of the wall where he had tried for a hold. Pat allowed his eyes to look upwards to the head snapped heavily to one side. The rope, he saw, was the new one, a clothes-line he himself had brought only days since, from Stones the ironmongers. He remembered the soft, silky feel of it, the pleasant tang of tallow.

He mixed milk from the larder with broken bread and watched the cat as she picked daintily at the food. Then, shaking his head from side to side in an effort to clear the buzzing sound that had started in his ears; he pulled the door shut behind him and set off for the mill. The cat followed him till he came to the corner shop, then she gave up, sat and began to wash herself with strong downward strokes.

His mother had been at The Egyptian all her working life and, now that the mills were shutting down, she thought herself lucky to get the little bit of employment that was still available and there was always a queue for the few jobs remaining.

Pat wound his way through the wet, familiar streets. He was aware of his progress; said hello to neighbours as he went, but he was in a mist, a cloud of soft cotton wool. He could not feel the pavement at his feet nor the ringing of his clog irons on the street. The buzzing in his ears persisted.

The great, red painted gates of the factory greeted him as he approached. There was an air of steam, hot oil and the clean, surprisingly pleasant smell of new cloth. Massive brick walls with hundreds of grimy windows surrounded the place. The tall, smoking chimney seemingly rooted in the worn cobbles of the yard with the name of the mill written large in white letters from top to bottom. A horse-drawn cart, laden with bobbins, nearly knocked Patrick down as he entered.

The time-keeper's office was just inside the gate. A commanding position from which he could observe the comings and goings of the work force. Life, in the immediate vicinity was ruled by the operations of the mill and you knew the hour by its various sights and sounds: At six in the morning the lonely step of one man, the fire-beater, made his way to the gates and his banked, steaming furnaces. At six forty five the hurried, worrying clogs of the spinners, the weavers, the carders.

The sprightly skip of the side and little piecers, just out of school and still happy with hope. At seven and just after, the disconsolate returning tread of the latecomers turned away at the gates for an enforced and unwelcome day off. The fire-bell tested at ten, then the dinner-time hooter and, at five in the evening the long drawn out siren for another day's ending.

'Mrs. Delaney? number six o seven that'll be,' the man was a face, tilted to one side, framed by the sides of his cubby-hole, a fag with a two inch ash on the end of it dangled wetly, brown-stained from loose lips as he squinted up at Pat:

'Only – I'll have to dock her; will she be long?' Pat waited silently, not knowing what he should say, till his mother came hot, flushed and angry to the little side door.

'What?' she demanded. 'What the bloody hell now? Turn me back for five minutes.....'

'Our dad,' Pat told her, 'he's hung hisself.'

Her wedding ring stung his ear as the blow landed. He reeled back against the factory wall.

'Little bugger – coming here with your bloody tales – I'm stopped a flaming hour because of you. Get to hell.' And Pat was half way up Draycott Street before he realized that the ringing in his ears had stopped.

CORPORATION CLOGS

●●●●●●●●●●●●●

'Bonny feet, them.' Patrick's Aunty said as she eyed him up over her newspaper. 'Crossed, and with a nail through, you'd look like Jesus.'

It was the clogs that did it, she assured him. Strengthened the sinews and highlighted the metatarsals. A bit of character, that's what you wanted for your feet and he, Patrick, had it. In spades she said.

All very well, Pat thought and alright for you to say, you don't have to wear them, nor, which was more to the point, have it known where they came from.

They were lounging in Pat's backyard, catching the bit of sun that had managed to penetrate the smog and the perpetual fine mist that belched from the concrete cooling towers of the local power station. A cat, lazy in the warm rays, jerked suddenly awake as the buzzing of a fly came too near its ears, causing it to swipe out with a paw, making a whole cloud of flies rise noisily from the midden on which it was trying to sleep.

'Middens,' mused Patrick. Outside lavatories, the stink of nearby factories and, on his feet, corporation clogs.

'Get you on.' His mother would say; 'we're going to the Co-op. I've got the entitlement and you can shut your mouth before you open it.'

Clogs! if only they were not so – obvious. Alright, they'd no money, not for clogs any way up. The Parish were very kind, he was grateful to them, but it was the way they did it that got Pat's goat: First it was the board, frowning down at you like you'd pinched one of their fat wallets:

'And when did your husband draw his last wages?' Husband! He'd gone out when Patrick came in and never a hair of him since. It was all Parish, the Provident Club and what bit she raked in for other folks washing.

And then came the Co-op. But not just any branch. Oh no! You had to go and queue at the Victory Yard. Notorious! Real scruffs most of them. Nits jumping from head to head, green snot dangling and when you got them, the clogs, they were grey. No nap, so, try as you might, you could never raise a polish and another thing - irons on the soles, never rubbers. Well, actually, irons were alright, they could hear you coming with irons on and you could always raise a spark or two to relieve the odd bit of boredom. Plus, when they wore down, fine and sharp at the edges, they could be very handy in a punch up. Everybody knew though, that was the rub:

'Here comes Pat in his corporation clogs.' They could tell them a mile away and he was sick to death of it.

'I've seen some shoes,' he told his Aunt: 'brown and I'm saving up to buy them.'

'Well,' she said, squinting again over the top of her paper: 'Let me be the first to congratulate you and I'll see it when I believe it.'

Pat looked at her. He was sure she was taking the mickey but, as usual with those that called themselves adult, you could never tell, so he just said 'right,' and went in to put his coat on.

The shop; Shipobotham's; was on the corner by The Lamb on Mona street. 'Everything,' it said over the window, 'Bought and Sold. Come in and Have a Look.' And there they were, amongst the chuck-outs from other people's houses: the dolly tubs, bicycles, prams, disused chamber pots, unused presents and last years diaries: nestled neat in their tissue papered box; one with its bottom uppermost revealing a brand new leather sole and heel: The shoes. Brogues – he had checked in his mother's catalogue and you could tell by the little bumps, like tiny pimples in the surface of the leather.

He went in and stood by the worn counter, littered with smaller items of bric-a-brac, invoices and a lonely fag, smouldering in a tin ash tray. 'Ring The Bell,' a sign said and he did as he was told, coughing discreetly to further advertise his presence.

'I'm coming,' a voice said – a woman's voice he noted with relief. Of the two – men and women, he found the latter the easiest to put up with. Though there wasn't much in it really, it was just that, him being so – pretty – as his Aunt described it; women tended to be a bit soft with him, till they knew him anyway:

'I'd give a tanner each for every last bat of them eyelashes,' one, a neighbour, was always telling him and she'd give his cheek a little stroke.

'How much,' said Patrick, 'the shoes,' and he nodded, as off-hand as he could at the items in question.

He had reckoned up: Ten bob a week for the paper round, that was two evening editions of The Evening News and, if he took on mornings that would be another five shillings, of which two thirds to his mam and of course he had to last through the week, one thing and another – ninepence at the Gem on Saturday mornings, he couldn't miss Flash Gordon and it was sixpence now at the public baths, bring your own soap too. Still, he could afford a couple of bob a week.

'Do you do tick?' he asked. She still hadn't answered his first question and she peered at him now, sideways. She looked, Pat thought, as though she were getting ready to eat him.

'Twelve shillings,' she finally said. 'For cash; fifteen on the never- never. Depends – how long are you thinking of?'

They eventually settled for twelve and six and Pat promised to have it paid up in four weeks. She would, meanwhile, keep the goods and put them by – was he looking for a suit incidentally: 'young lad same build as you, went down with scarlet fever, only worn once.'

Patrick viewed life, generally speaking, as a bit of a puzzle. If you fancied something for instance it was more or less certain that, for one reason or another, you couldn't have it and, on the other hand, whenever you had made your mind up to detest a thing and made every effort to stay clear of it, then, sure enough, up it would creep when you were looking the other way and clout you, bang beside the ear.

Waiting was not his favourite pastime and so, week by dragging week he took in his remittance to Mrs. Shipobotham, his clogs meanwhile getting heavier and louder, his toes crying out for what he knew for sure would be the gentle caress of real, genuine leather.

He made sure that his mates knew what he was up to. Partly anyway: 'I'm getting to old for clogs me mam says – she's looking out for a nice pair of brogues. Any day now,' and of he would go flushed with the joy of, for once, getting what he wanted.

Saturday night was pay night. It was also the night of the heaviest load newspaper-wise. The Buff came out at five followed by the Green Final at half past six. This last was dedicated to all the results of the day's sport and it always seemed to Pat that just about everybody in town wanted one. His bag was a ton weight as he left the shop but he could not help but hum a little tune as he went along and his step was light with anticipation. The only draw back was all day tomorrow – Sunday, stretching endlessly before him. He had the last of the money, counted it a dozen times, two more shillings and the shoes were his.

It was a dry day that Monday morning and he was glad of that as it would do the leather good to get some wear in before the rain came down. He was there at nine just as Mrs Shipobotham came out with her long pole to wind down the awning.

'Expecting some sun then I see,' Pat said brightly. You never knew- she might knock a few bob off. He was not really surprised when she didn't:

'Two bob to settle,' she demanded, fist out like a claw as he counted out the coins. 'Here you are,' she said, 'and I've thrown in new laces for nowt.'

Patrick fairly flew through the streets, his clogs ringing their own death knell on the paving stones beneath his feet. In at the back gate, alarming the cat in his hurry, up the bare wooden stairs clunk – clunk, to the sanctuary of his bed-room where he literally threw off the offending clogs, turned his socks round so no hole showed, and on with the shoes, the smell of `warm leather keen in his nostrils, the gentle yet firm grip as he tightened the laces. He sat on the bed looking down at them, his heart nearly bursting with pride. At last. Proper shoes.

His mother was stirring something on the stove as he went down to the kitchen, her hair loose over her worried forehead.

'I hope you've made your bed this morning,' she said, 'and you can go to Flitcroft's in a minute; we've no bread.'

'What do you think?' he said to her, doing a little pirouette on the lino, his feet tap tapping in a dance.

'Think?' she said, considering, 'well, I think they are very nice but – and she paused, her voice suddenly softening as she looked at him -why didn't you get a lad's pair? them's girl's shoes.'

A COLD WIND

●●●●●●●●●●●●

At the rear of the derelict church, approached by an underground tunnel, is a storage space or warehouse. A cobbled court yard, mediaeval in origin, is set in the middle of these outbuildings. Old pews are kept there, massive oak structures, crumbling with age and easily broken up. Tramps have made their home there as well as local drunks their party venue. A fire burns almost constantly in an old oil drum which is fed from the pile of ready timber and supplemented from surrounding bombed out houses and factories. The occupants, transient and some more permanent, live out their lives there, unaffected by or maybe in spite of, the war going on around them. Indeed, some of them have had their war already and this is what it has brought them too.

'Do you realize,' says Doctor Johnson, fag end wet, brown stained in cracked lips. 'That bleeding wind has nothing to stop it, one way or another, east or west, top or bottom, from here to – what?' and he indicates vaguely the cardinal points of an imaginary compass.

'North – a – bloody merica, your Rockies. Up there's your Urals or one of them. The Alps, and down there,' pointing to the space between his feet, 'fuck knows. A long drop, that's for sure.' The light from the fire dances across the hard shadows of his face: 'Antarctic probably.' He removes the dimp from between his teeth, spits on the oil drum glowing dull red:

'That's drawing good any way up – pews burn well – all them greasy fat arses rubbing up and down in praise of The Lord.' He crosses himself as, with the other hand he chucks on another splintered plank to make the bright sparks soar skyward through a hole in the hammered ceiling above them.

Lizzie, tiny, almost transparent, hutches closer to the fire on an old stained mattress. She watches the leaping lights, her own eyes just as bright and with a simple wonder in them.

'Jewels,' she whispers. 'Look how they gleam, rushing up so fast and dying. How...?' and here she turns to Doc,....'did the prayers get out? when it was still a church I mean,' she adds quickly so as not to be scorned. Too late of course for Doc's lips already sneer. The girl cringes, expecting a blow but the Doc only smiles at her good naturedly.

'Simple little bugger, ain't you?' and the girl smiles back, sighs and settles herself among the newspapers crinkling around her legs.

By the fire, the Deacon is mixing the tonic, his hands, for the time being, the steadiest. Released only that day from St. Catherine's, he has emineverin in hand to taper down with, he has, he knows, eight pills left and he is tempted as always to swallow the lot. His arse is still sore after the twelve thick shots, six each cheek, of vitamins. Stooped now, he is less tall than when named but he still manages to appear sepulchral. A cracked, cadaverous face. Filthy nails on fine pianists hands. His stretched, striding gait. The black calf length coat: A preacher, that's what he looks like – and becomes, given half a chance. Keen as a chemist now and no drop spilt, he measures the linctus and mixes the cocktail. Two flagons of cider and one bottle of cough mixture, these, the last purchase out of their combined daily dole are all they have left between them, unless there is a miracle, until late the next morning. Meths, of course – they have meths. A pint bottle from the iron monger, purple dye notwithstanding, stowed behind the ruined altar. Just in case.

The Deacon, taking the first swift swig from one of the cider bottles, passes it, almost reverently to the girl.

'Only a wet,' he warns, but gently as Lizzie, sinews tight against the savage shaking of her head, tilts and gulps. Then the Doc, mouth chewing, savouring, swallowing his morsel. He belches wetly.

'Ex - act,' he pronounces and, holding the bottle up to the fire light – 'spike it milord,' he says. 'Liven the fucker.' and the Deacon pours the syrup in.

The neat smell of the mixture, overcoming that of the wood smoke, is too much for the girl. She begins to retch, trembling violently, dry, sobbing heaves rack and rail her frail frame. Tears flood her death-white cheeks as the spasms grip her.

'Ether,' says the Deacon, 'that's what does it, the smell – morphine or whatever. Here, go on,' and he holds the bottle to the girl's lips again, steadying, as best he can, the pumping of her head. 'Teeth, for fuck's sake, mind your teeth.' The girl lies on her side, exhausted and the Doc covers her up, using his own coat.

'That'll settle her,' Doc says as, gradually, the shuddering eases, slows, stops, until only an occasional wave, a small electric shock, remains.

Doctor Johnson rises unsteadily to his feet, casting a looming black shadow, ghost - like among the ruins. He begins a little dance.

'Syrataki,' he tells them. 'Picked it up in Greece whilst serving...'

'Yeah, yeah, we know,' says Deacon. 'With the bloody partisans.'

The Doc pauses. He eyes his friend evenly, directly.

'That's correct,' he murmurs, 'abso bloody lutely.' and he takes up the dance again, pirouetting and stomping his feet on the flags and the centuries old gravestones, arms outstretched, faster and faster, until he collapses in a heap on his mattress.

The girl is calmer now, the shaking has almost stopped and she is able to think more clearly. She worries about the boys: Deacon and Doc. Her good friends. Protectors even, for there are many about who would be only too ready to take advantage. She is an old fashioned girl and, at thirty and despite the ravages of the alcohol, she is, and she knows she is, sexually attractive.

Doc is looking at her now. She knows that look, just as she knows that The Deacon is watching them. Both. There exists a caginess between the two men. They are wary of each other and she knows that the reason for it is herself. She knows the true depth of their friendship, their loyalty to each other. She stands between them now and does not know what to do.

Early, very early, next morning, there is a scuffling in the courtyard. It is not yet daylight. Men's voices are heard. Flashlights pierce the darkness.

'Who's here?' a voice demands. 'Deacon? Doc?' It is the agency; the so called ships husbands. They are looking for crew and Deacon and Doc cringe low in their bedding.

'One of you, that's all. Any one. Cook on the Freebooter, sailing at seven and we need you now. Deacon? – Doc?'

It is Deacon who goes. It's his turn and in any case, having just been dried out, he is the fittest. He does not want to go. The thought of steaming up the East coast. The cold, foul North Sea. The withdrawals, the inevitable spewing. Thirty to seventy days on station. But, then, there's the money. They need the money. He stands looking down at them both; a man, and a woman, his friends, curled in their warm beds. The agents have left the engine running in the van. He picks up his bag. They sound their horn.

'Okay. Okay.' He says and suddenly laughs. 'Life.' He says and strides without looking back, through the door and out into the still sleeping street.

A DEATH IN THE FAMILY

●●●●●●●●●●●●●

'Your Kenny's dead.' Spud Murphy, down in the street, had his hands cupped to his mouth. Pat was on top of the ladder which was leant against the gable end wall of Sam's Family Butchers. 'Quality Meats. Best Cuts.' He continued painting. It had been expected. He had only the front left to do, might as well finish it. Three coats all in all, inside and out of the troughings plus barge boards and fascias. It was his usual job when they were on outsides, summertime and it paid well, piece work.

He lowered the ladder down into itself, laid it horizontal against the wall. He scraped his brushes dry of paint and placed them carefully into a few inches of water in a can. Keep them soft till next time. Splashing a few drops of turps on top of the paint to stop skinning, he put everything away in the little shed at the top of the yard.

The linseed oil smelt lovely as he massaged it into his hands. Dried with a twist of cotton waste, his fingers and palms came up soft and pink. He took off his white overalls which, he noticed, could do with a wash. He hung them on a hook on the wall and, bolting the gate behind him, he set off for home.

The coffin was under the window. Pat, getting ready for work that morning, had heard Ken struggling for breath. The mother had been sat by the bed which had been brought down from the back bedroom weeks ago now. She had been staring into space, a cold cup of tea clasped in her two hands. The rasping, bubbling sound had persisted as Pat washed at the kitchen sink. He had wondered to himself at the reality of that strange noise, the death rattle, which, if anything, he had thought of as a fiction.

The little room was full of relatives. Aunties mainly. The one he knew best, Edith, his father's sister, put her arm around his shoulder.

'Now then,' she said, 'brave soldier. That's it,' and, leading him into the kitchen, she sat him down to his tea which she had made ready and placed on a tray on top of the kitchenette.

'There's another cup when you want it,' she told him, 'and then you must have a little look. He looks really bonny.'

'Pernicious Anaemia,' another Aunt told everybody. She was already in black and had very large bosoms. 'They know next to nothing about it yet and there they are talking about a second front. All that money on war....... You'll have to buck up you know.' This to Pat's mother, crouched by the fire. 'It does no good and he'll want his tea when he comes in.'

'I won't look,' Pat told them. They stood, two or three of them including Edith, surrounding the casket. The lid was on the floor beneath the coffin which was suspended at each end on two chairs he recognised as part of next doors dining suite, the Pattersons, with whom, as far as he knew, his family were not on speaking terms.

'Oh. You must look,' said one of the Aunts, 'you'll never forgive yourself. Have a quick peep – he's only sleeping.'

They had walked up Stantons by the lakes, a crowd of them. Both Tyldsleys, Sammy with the wall eye, Billy Fogg. Kenny had lagged behind over the big field which sloped upward and was always muddy under foot. Hard going but they had pressed on while Kenny, white faced, labouring for breath, staggered and stood, his arms open hopelessly, staring up at them as they turned and looked down towards him.

'Leave him,' said Billy, who was a kind of leader. 'Too bloody slow to catch a cold,' which wasn't true at all since Kenny caught everything – Scarlet Fever, Mumps, Whooping Cough - but they did leave him behind and Pat among them.

'You're never going out,' his Aunty Edith said. But 'Yes, I am,' he told her and off he went catching the tram at the corner and down to Bridge street and The Paladium.

They had taken out the soft velvet seats due to vandalism and he welcomed the cold hardness of the aluminium. He pressed himself down onto the unyielding surface in the dark. Pulling upwards with his hands. The hard edge of the seat cutting in on the backs of his knees, shutting off the blood, causing his legs to throb painfully. Later, walking back up Bridge street, the trams whizzing past on squealing, sparking wheels, the smell of chips and the taste of fog, he could not remember anything at all about the film.

Next morning everybody was in their best. Black ties and some of the women had veils on.

'Are you sure?' Edith asked him again, the man poised with the lid held high. Pat turned away. He could not, would not look. The screws squeaked down and they lifted the coffin into the hearse.

Crowds lined the route. It was only a short way to St. Thomas's and they were mostly folk known to them as a family. Men held their trilbies or flat caps to their chests. The bell doled out its misery.

Suffer little children. All things bright and beautiful. Ashes to ashes. Men blew their noses while women wept. Pat watched the dust motes bounding and billowing in a sharp shaft of coloured light that pierced the sadness and lit up the lilies on the polished lid.

It rained in the graveyard. Someone held an umbrella over the vicar in his white and black surplice and they had to forcibly prevent Pat's mother from leaping into the hole.

'Shows you up,' said the Aunty with big bosoms and, noticing Uncle Tom at the fringes with his bright red cheeks and overhanging belly: 'He's had a few and not ten o-clock yet. Shocking.'

The Co-op Small Hall was up some stairs and above the office where Pat and Ken had queued for the divvy, years ago now it seemed.

Tongue sandwiches, Tizer and Brown ale. A big urn of tea and their father telling jokes about the clippie and room for one more on top.

Gradually, everybody dispersed and Pat and his family caught the number eight bus which was just across the road. At home, the blinds were still drawn. The father swept them apart.

'Get that spanner,' the man told his son. 'It's in the shed somewhere. We'll get this bed shifted.'

Printed in the United Kingdom
by Lightning Source UK Ltd.
120856UK00001B/339